Jane Yolen

Welcome to the ICE HOUSE

Illustrated by Laura Regan

G. P. Putnam's Sons · New York

With thanks to Dr. Joe Cooke and Carolyn Parker,
of the University of Alaska Museum in Fairbanks

Text copyright © 1998 by Jane Yolen · Illustrations copyright © 1998 by Laura Regan
All rights reserved. This book, or parts thereof, may not be reproduced in any form without
permission in writing from the publisher. G. P. Putnam's Sons, a division of
The Putnam & Grosset Group, 200 Madison Avenue, New York, NY 10016.
G. P. Putnam's Sons, Reg. U.S. Pat. & Tm. Off. Published simultaneously in Canada.
Printed in Hong Kong by South China Printing Co. (1988) Ltd. Text set in Meridien Medium.

Library of Congress Cataloging-in-Publication Data
Yolen, Jane. Welcome to the ice house / Jane Yolen; illustrated by Laura Regan.   p.   cm.
Summary: The coming of warm weather to the arctic brings an explosion of color from flowering
plants and a thundering return of wildlife.   1. Zoology—Arctic regions—Juvenile literature.
2. Seasons—Arctic regions—Juvenile literature.   [1. Zoology—Arctic regions.
2. Arctic regions.]   I. Regan, Laura, ill.   II. Title.   QL105.Y65   1998   591.7586
[E]—DC21   97-9609   CIP   AC   ISBN 0-399-23011-4
10 9 8 7 6 5 4 3 2 1   FIRST IMPRESSION

For Refna, who has always made me welcome.
—JY

For Burt Brent, fellow artist and great friend.
Thank you for your encouragement.
—LR

Welcome to the ice house,
the snow and wintry blow house,
where shades of white
illuminate
the lengthy winter night.

Where well below the snowscape
caper lemmings in long tunnels,
racing through the runnels
to escape
the singular arctic fox
on the prowl

or the howling wolf pack
sniffing out the track
of snowshoe hare
or ptarmigan
white as wintertide.
But beware.

Beware, for behind
stalks a lynx,
now quick, now slow,
now silent as snow.

But all give way—
fox, lemming, lynx, hare—
to a ton of unpredictable moose
on the loose

or the hungry, tireless polar bear.

Yet this is not just a landscape of snow,
blue sky above, ice below.
The Arctic seas are blue and black.
Beyond the ice crack
swim gray and brown seals:
spotted seal, ringed seal, and harp.

And slickly black,
sleekly white,
hunting through the lengthy Arctic night,
sure as an arrow's arc
along the ocean trails,
south of the ice
come the streamlined killer whales.

Here, too, swim dense herds,
immense herds,
of baggy-skinned,
saggy-skinned,
rust-colored walrus
strutting ivory tusks for defense.

Above in the sky,
gyrfalcon sails;
down below, beluga whales,
singing like giant birds,
welcoming
the return of a moment
of spring.

For—as if on a single day—
spring and summer return together.

The weather softens, warms,
and swarms of poppies and lupine
burst open, grow;
an explosion of color
where once grew only ice and snow.

Then caribou with hooves like thunder
cross the tundra;

and the grizzly rises from its winter nap,
grubbing roots,
grabbing voles
and other small mammals from their holes.

Birds return, too,
to iceless lakes and snowless cliffs:
swans, puffins, loons,
and arctic terns,
who journey from pole to pole
to rest,
to nest.

And then—brief moment—
summer is gone.
Winter comes again
and lingers on and on and on

in the cold house,
the ice house,
the snow and wintry blow house.
Welcome to the ice house
and the long winter night.

Did You Know?

The area of the far north beyond the tree line is known as the Arctic. Once it was called the "frigid zone" and the "barren lands." Non-natives believed that nothing could possibly live or grow there.

The word "arctic" comes from the Greek *arktos*, which means "bear." This does not mean the polar bear or the grizzly or any real bear that travels across the snowscape. Rather, it refers to the northern constellation called the Bear.

What do we find in the Arctic? An enormous difference in temperatures between summer and winter, certainly. In the high country of the Arctic, as well as at sea level in Greenland and in the Canadian archipelago, there is permanent ice and snow. But more than three-fifths of the Arctic thaws in the summer under a continuous sun that never actually sets. This is the land of the long summer day. And in the Arctic summer there is a wonderful flowering of plants and a thundering return of wildlife.

Then winter sets in again, the long night that is both white and cold. An ice house, indeed.

To find out more about the Arctic, contact:

University of Alaska Museum
907 Yukon Drive
PO Box 756960
Fairbanks, AK 99775-6960

web site:http://www.uaf.alaska.edu/museum